For John Thacher Hurd

When he comes

(He's here)

My World
Copyright © 1949 by Harper & Brothers
Text copyright © renewed 1977 by Roberta Brown Rauch, executrix
Illustrations copyright © renewed 1977 by Clement Hurd
New color palette copyright © 2001 by Thacher Hurd
Printed in the U.S.A. All rights reserved.
www.harperchildrens.com

Library of Congress Cataloging-in-Publication Data
Brown, Margaret Wise.
    My world / by Margaret Wise Brown ; pictures by Clement Hurd.
        p.   cm.
    Summary: A little bunny delights in all the familiar things in his daily life.
    ISBN 0-06-024798-3 — ISBN 0-06-024799-1 (lib. bdg.)
    [1. Rabbits—Fiction. 2. Family life—Fiction.] I. Hurd, Clement, ill.
II. Title.
PZ7.B8163 My 1995   94025755
[E]—20   CIP
                                                                    AC

1 2 3 4 5 6 7 8 9 10
❖

My book. Mother's book.
In my book I only look.

The fire burns.

The pages turn.

Mother's chair.
My chair.
   A low chair.
   A high chair.
   But certainly my chair.

Daddy's slippers.
My slippers.
My pajamas.
Daddy's pajamas.
Even my teddy bear
Wears pajamas.

My dog.
Daddy's dog.
Daddy's dog
Once caught a frog.

My spoon.
Daddy's spoon.
"The moon belongs
To the man in the moon."

Daddy's boy.
Mother's boy.
My boy is just a toy
Bear.

My car.
Daddy's car.

Bang Bang Bang—My ca[r]

My car won't go very far.

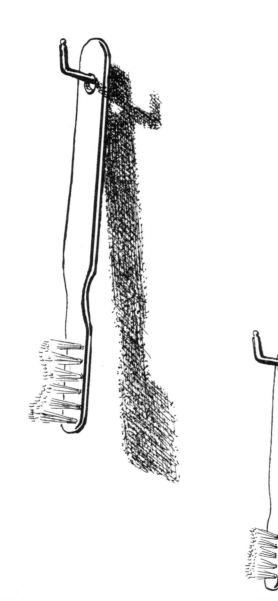
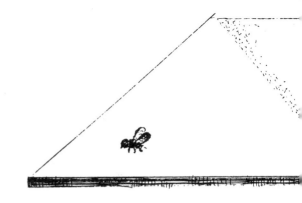

My toothbrush.
Daddy's toothbrush.

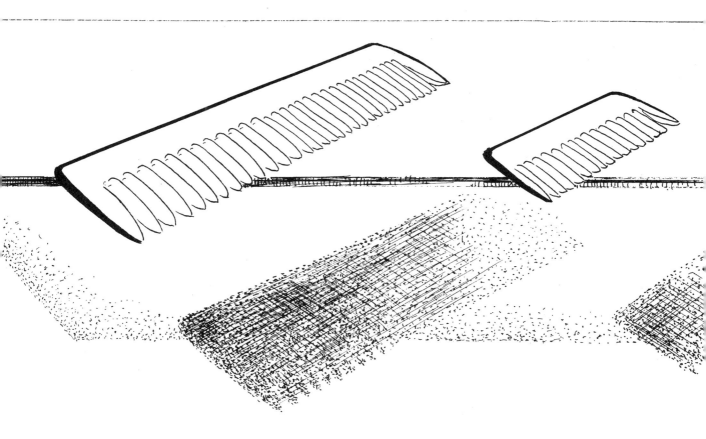

My comb.
Mother's comb.

My soap. Daddy's soap.

My soap will make soapsuds, I hope.

My fish.
Daddy's fish.
When you catch
A fish you make
A wish.

My bed.
Mother's bed.
I go to sleep
When my story is read,
When my prayers are said,
And when my head
Is sleepy on the pillow.

My breakfast.
My morning.
Daddy's breakfast.
Good morning.

My kitty.
Daddy's kitty.
Daddy's kitty
Has gone to the city.

Your world.
My world.

I can swing
Right over the world.

My tree.

The bird's tree.

How many stripes
On a bumble bee?